To
The Covenant School Library

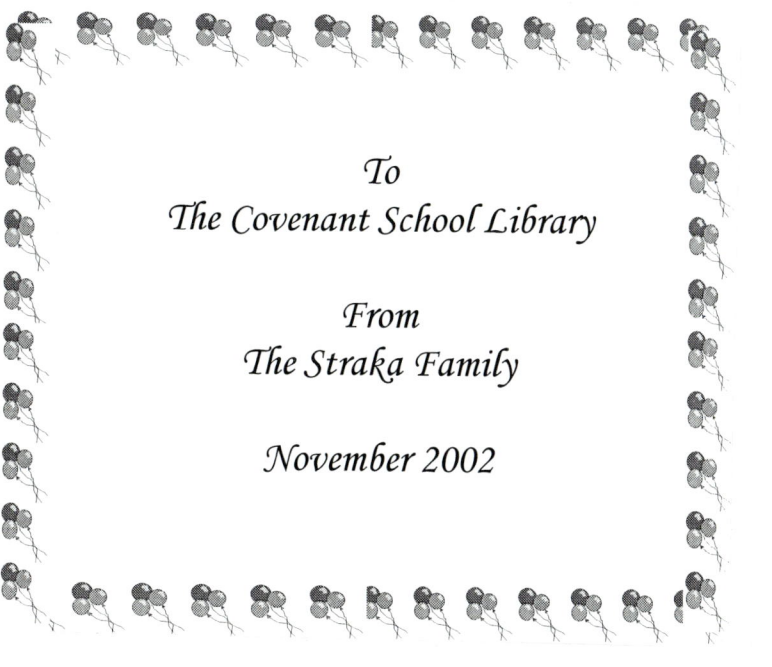

From
The Straka Family

November 2002

Taking Your Camera to
CANADA

Ted Park

Steadwell Books

Raintree Steck-Vaughn Publishers

A Harcourt Company

Austin · New York
www.steck-vaughn.com

Copyright © 2000, Steck-Vaughn Company

All rights reserved. No part of this book may be reproduced or utilized in any form or by any means, electronic or mechanical, including photocopying, recording, or by any information storage and retrieval system, without permission in writing from the publisher. Inquiries should be addressed to copyright permissions, Steck-Vaughn Company, P.O. Box 26015, Austin, TX 78755.

Published by Raintree Steck-Vaughn Publishers,
an imprint of Steck-Vaughn Company

Library of Congress Cataloging-in-Publication Data
Park, Ted
  Canada / by Ted Park.
      p. cm. — (Taking your camera to)
   Summary: Introduces the geography, points of interest, way of life, economy, culture, and people of Canada.
   ISBN 0-7398-1803-1
   1. Canada—Juvenile literature. 2. Canada—Pictorial works—Juvenile literature. 3. Historic sites—Canada—Juvenile literature. [1. Canada.] I. Title: Canada. II. Series.

F1008.2.P37 2000
971—dc21   99-057515

Printed in the United States of America
10 9 8 7 6 5 4 3 2 1 W 03 02 01 00

Photo acknowledgments

Cover ©Yoyohiro Yamada/FPG International; pp.1, 3a ©Burgess Blevins/FPG International; p.3b ©Peter Gridley/FPG International; p.3c ©Toyohiro Yamada/FPG International; p.3d ©Walter Bibikow/FPG International; p.4 ©Keith Gunnar/FPG International; p.5 ©Ron Thomas/FPG International; p.8 ©Peter Gridley/FPG International; p.9 ©Toyohiro Yamada/FPG International; p.11 ©Walter Bibikow/FPG International; p.12 ©Peter Gridley/FPG International; p.13 ©Walter Bibikow/FPG International; p.15 ©Burgess Blevins/FPG International; p.17 ©Paul A. Souders/CORBIS; p.19 ©Corbis; p.21 ©PhotoDisc; p.23a ©Scott Markewitz/FPG International; p.23b ©Corbis RF; p.25a ©PhotoDisc; p.25b ©PhotoDisc; p.25c ©PhotoDisc; p.27 ©AP Photo/Eric Draper; p.28a ©Corbis; p.28b ©Ron Thomas/FPG International; p.29a ©PhotoDisc; p.29b ©Walter Bibikow/FPG International; p.29c ©Keith Gunnar/FPG International.

All statistics in the Quick Facts section come from *The New York Times Almanac* (1999) and *The World Almanac* (1999).

Contents

This Is Canada	4
The Place	6
Quebec City	10
Places to Visit	12
The People	14
Life in Canada	16
Government and Religion	18
Earning a Living	20
School and Sports	22
Food and Holidays	24
The Future	26
Quick Facts About Canada	28
Glossary	30
Index	32

This Is Canada

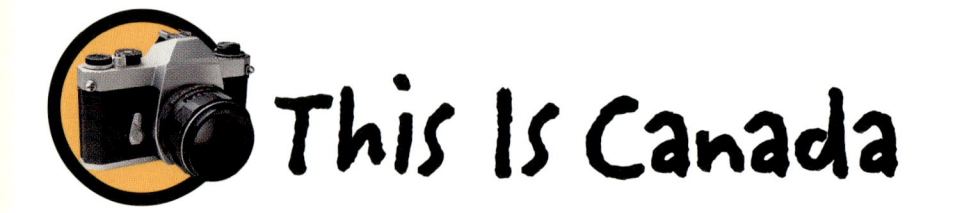

Canada is a huge country. It has tall mountains and deep lakes. It has grassy plains and thick forests. And in one part of the country it is winter all the time. If you took your camera to Canada, you would be able to take photographs of all kinds of places.

Canada is divided into provinces and territories, which are like states. Canada has many interesting cities. One of them is Vancouver, in the province of British Columbia. This is Canada's largest city on the Pacific coast.

The Rocky Mountains in western Canada

A night scene in Victoria

If you walked around Vancouver, you could take photographs of old buildings.

This book will show you some of the different lands and places in Canada. It will also tell you much about the country of Canada. By knowing about Canada before you take your camera there, you will enjoy your visit more.

The Place

Canada is the second-largest country in the world. Only Russia is bigger. Canada is about 2,500 miles (4,000 km) from north to south. From east to west it is 3,426 miles (5,513 km). This is about half the size of North America. Canada is slightly larger than the entire United States.

Canada has many types of land. The Rocky Mountains are in the west. In the east are the Appalachian Mountains. In between them are the prairies. These are large areas of grassy plains. This is where most of Canada's farms are. Half of Canada is covered with forests. To the far north the land is always frozen. That is because northern Canada is only about 500 miles (805 km) from the North Pole.

Canada has oceans on three of its borders. To the north is the Arctic Ocean. The Atlantic Ocean is to the east. And the Pacific Ocean is to the west. To the south of Canada is the United States.

Artic Ocean
United States
Beaufort Sea
Tuktoyaktuk
Baffin Bay
Ikateq
Godthab
Na
Whitehorse
Great Bear Lake
Port Radium
Juneau
Yellowknife
Great Slave Lake
Baker Lake
Labrador Sea
N
Rankin Inlet
Bear Lake
Prince Rupert
Fort Chipewyan
Dawson Creek
Grande Prairie
Fort McMurray
Churchill
Hudson Bay
Inukjuak
Edmonton
Thompson
Flin Flon
Kamloops
Red Deer
Labrador City
Vancouver
North Battleford
Prince Albert
Kelowna
Calgary
Corner Brook
Trail
Saskatoon
Lake Winnipeg
Lethbridge
Moosonee
Gulf of St. Lawrence
Regina
CANADA
Brandon
Winnipeg
Amos
Charlottetown
Thunder Bay
Timmins
Quebec
Fredericton
Bismarck
Lake Superior
Trois-rivieres
Halifax
Sudbury
North Bay
Montreal
Augusta
Ottawa
Yarmouth
Lake Huron
Kingston
St. Paul
Lake Michigan
Toronto
Montpelier
UNITED STATES
Lake Ontario
Concord
Albany
Boston
Madison
Lansing
Hartford
Atlantic Ocean
Lake Erie
Cheyenne
Des Moines
Canada
National Capital
Calgary
City
International Boundary
Provincial Boundary
Quebec
Province Name
500 km
0
500 Miles

Fishing boats in a harbor on Cape Breton Island

Canada's rivers and lakes hold one-seventh of the world's freshwater. Hudson Bay is in central Canada. A bay is a body of water that is almost totally surrounded by land. Hudson Bay is very big. It is 281,900 square miles (730,064 sq km).

Four of the five Great Lakes separate parts of Canada and the United States. Thousands of ships sail on the lakes each year.

One of the most famous waterfalls in the world is on the Great Lakes. This is Niagara Falls. The part of the falls that is in Canada is called Horseshoe Falls. Many people come from all over the world to see the falls.

Canada has some of the coldest weather in the world. In the winter the average temperature is 0° F (-18° C). Then, snow covers much of the country.

Niagara Falls and the *Maid of the Mist* tourist boat

Quebec City

Quebec City is the oldest city in Canada. People have lived there for about 500 years. If you took your camera to Quebec City, you could take photographs of the city's narrow streets and squares. A square is an open area surrounded by buildings. You could also photograph some of its old buildings.

During Quebec City's early days, the Place Royale was the main area for people to shop and do business. On one side of it is a church called Nôtre-Dame-des-Victoires. The church was built in 1688. It is one of the oldest churches in Canada.

Quebec City has a walkway that goes along one side of the city. From there you can take pictures of the St. Lawrence River. You can also take pictures of the Château Frontenac. The Château Frontenac is a very big hotel that stands high above the river. It is one of the most famous sights in Quebec City.

The Château Frontenac in Quebec City. It is a famous hotel high above the city.

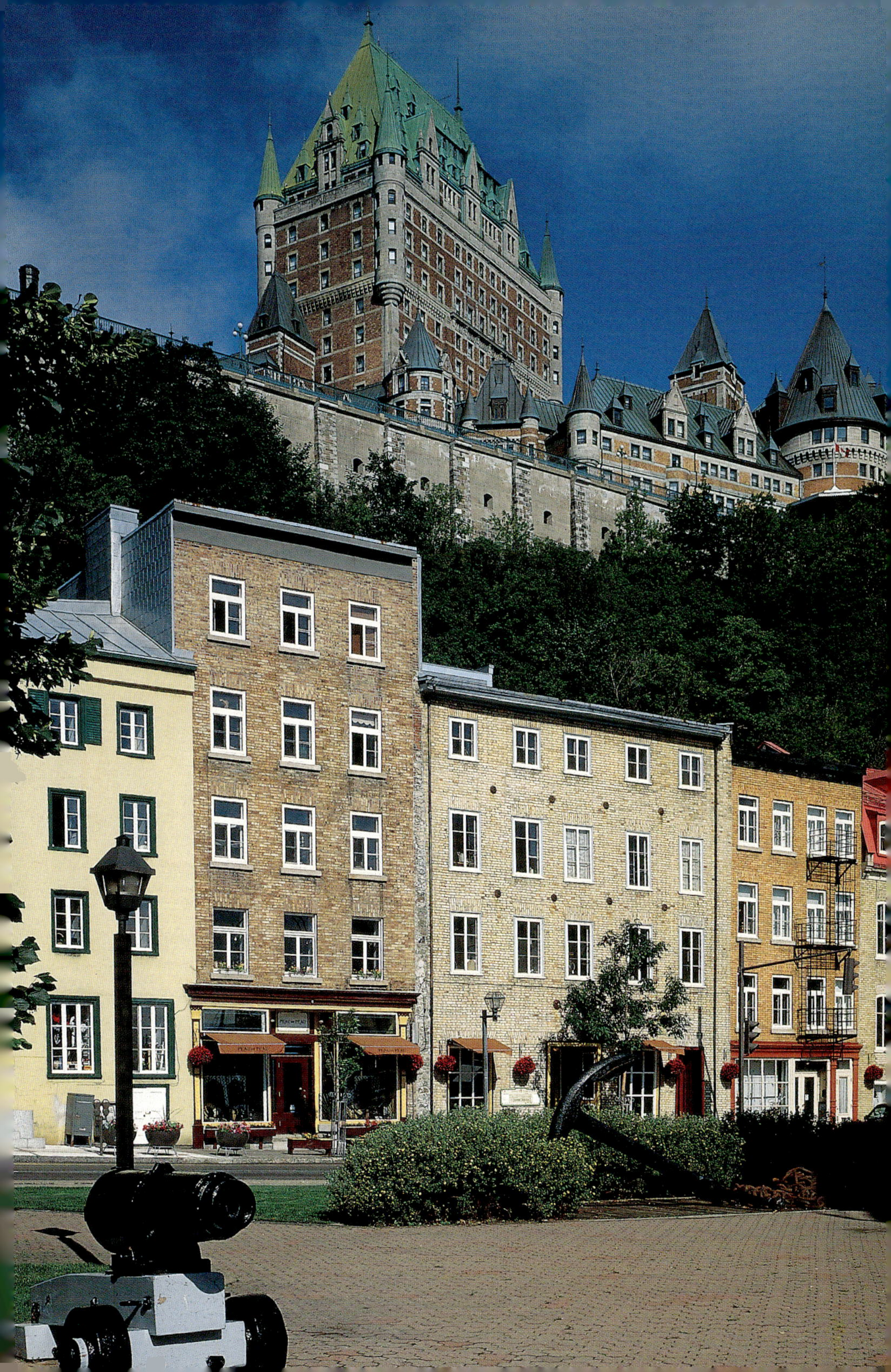

Places to Visit

The French came to Canada in the 1700s. Many people became trappers, who sold animal fur. Montreal was the center of this fur trade. Montreal is in the province of Quebec. Today most people who live in Montreal still speak French. A well-known place in the old part of the city is Jacques Cartier Place. This was named for the French explorer who came to eastern Canada in 1534. Montreal also has many big buildings, stores, and restaurants.

Jacques Cartier Place, in Montreal

The CN Tower in Toronto is 1,821 feet (555 m) high.

The British also came to Canada. Great Britain and France fought over Canada for almost a hundred years. Great Britain won, and many British people moved to Canada.

Toronto is the center of English-speaking Canada. It is in the province of Ontario. Toronto is Canada's largest city and is an important center of business. A well-known sight in the city is the Canadian National Tower, or CN Tower for short.

The People

There are more than 30 million people living in Canada. This is not a big number of people for a country as large as Canada. That is because almost no one lives in parts of the frozen north. Most Canadians come from either British or French backgrounds.

The first people who lived in Canada were probably Native Americans and Inuit. There are about 800,000 Native Americans and about 27,000 Inuits living in Canada. Inuits are people who live in the Arctic area. Most Native Americans and Inuit live in the Northwest Territories.

In 1993 the Canadian government set aside land for Inuits and other Native Americans. They used land from the Northwest Territories. The land became known as Nunavut in 1999.

Over time people from other countries have come to Canada to look for jobs and to earn more money.

Inuit children

Some of these people have come from Europe and some from Asia.

Life in Canada

More than half of all Canadians live in the provinces of Quebec and Ontario. These people live within 200 miles (320 km) of the U.S. border. In the province of Quebec, 82 percent of the people speak French. In most of the rest of Canada, the people speak English.

Most Canadians live in cities. In about half of Canadian families, both parents work. Many have good jobs and are well paid. Because of this they can enjoy their vacation time. In Canada the summers are short, so people make the most of them. They may take trips across Canada. Good roads and fast trains make travel easy. The Trans-Canada Highway runs across Canada. From east to west, it is the longest highway in the world. It is 4,860 miles (7,821 km) long.

Many tourists frequent Canada's numerous campsites in recreational vehicles.

Government and Religion

Canada is a federation with a parliamentary democracy. A federation means that the ten provinces and three territories that make up Canada joined together into one country. A democracy means that the people vote for their leaders.

Parliament is the name of Canada's ruling body. Parliament is made up of the Senate and the House of Commons. The prime minister is the head of the government. The prime minister has many advisers. Canada still has many ties to Great Britain.

Canada's police force is called the Royal Canadian Mounted Police. They are also called the "Mounties." The red uniforms they wear are well known all over the world. The Mounties keep law and order, especially in rural areas.

Ottawa's government buildings are next to the Rideau Canal.

Ottawa is Canada's capital. It is in southeast Ontario, on the Ottawa River. Founded in 1827, it became the capital in 1858. Almost one million people live there. Parliament buildings, the Royal Mint, and the National Art Gallery are in Ottawa. Rideau Canal freezes over in the winter, and people skate there.

Nearly half of all Canadians are Roman Catholics. About a third of the people are Protestants. There are also small groups of Jews, Muslims, Hindus, and Buddhists.

Earning a Living

In Canada people have many different kinds of jobs. Some people make their living by farming. Canada grows 16 percent of the world's wheat. In eastern Canada there are dairy farms, and in the west cattle are raised. Fishing is an important industry, especially on the coasts.

Some Canadians make their livings by mining, or digging up, Canada's many natural resources. A natural resource is something that comes from nature and is useful to people. Canada's major natural resources are oil and coal. The country also has many minerals. These include zinc, uranium, lead, iron ore, gold, and silver.

Because Canada has so many forests, there is plenty of wood. Some of the wood is cut into lumber. Some is made into paper. The forests are also homes for elk, moose, and bears. Some Native Americans and Inuit trade furs and skins for a living.

Grain crops are grown on Canada's western prairies.

The car industry brings jobs to people. Tourism is also important. Many people earn their livings by working in hotels and stores. And, because Canada is a growing country, there is work for builders.

School and Sports

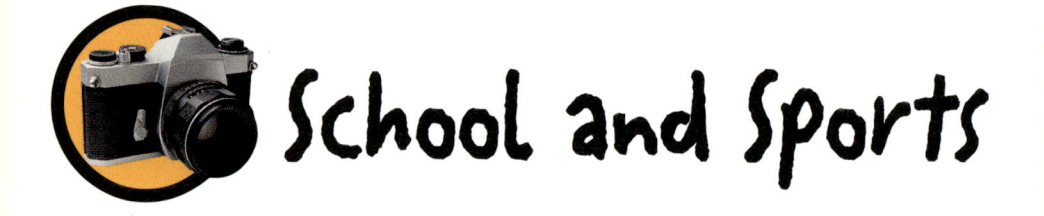

More young people in Canada go to schools and colleges than in any other country. They must go to school from ages 6 to 16. Each province has its own school system. Most schools are run by the government. Young people who want to go to college must stay in school until they are 18. Then they may take exams to get into college.

Because of Canada's climate, many sports are played in cold weather. Ice hockey is Canada's most popular sport. Canadians play it from an early age. Children learn to skate when they are very young. Skiing is also popular in many places.

Baseball is enjoyed as well. In western Canada, the rodeo is popular. The Calgary Stampede is held each year in the province of Alberta. A stampede is a kind of rodeo. Because Canada has so much wildlife, many people fish and hunt.

Skiing and skating are popular in Canada.

Food and Holidays

Canadians eat food much like their neighbors in the United States. Those who live near water eat fish. Those who live in the plains tend to eat meat, which is plentiful. Because of this, dishes of meat, fish, and other seafood are popular in Canada. Canadians also use grain crops for food. People in French-speaking Canada like French bread and other kinds of French food. Canadians eat plenty of fruits and vegetables.

Canada Day is an important holiday in Canada. It is on July 1. Canadians celebrate Thanksgiving Day every year just as Americans do. The first Thanksgiving days in both countries were harvest festivals. People gave thanks for the good crops they had. Canada's Thanksgiving Day is held on the second Monday of October. This is about six weeks earlier than the U.S. holiday. Most Canadians are Christians. Their major holidays are Christmas and Easter.

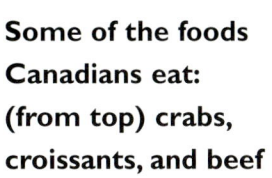

Some of the foods Canadians eat: (from top) crabs, croissants, and beef

The Future

If you took your camera to Canada, you would see a modern industrial country. An industrial country is one that makes goods. Unlike some other industrial countries, Canada has clean air and water.

Canada is rich in natural resources. When Canada exports, or sends, them to other countries, this brings money into the country. This also makes jobs for many Canadians. Most of the Canadian people earn enough money to buy food and other things they need to live.

Canada's biggest problem comes from within. There has always been a struggle in Canada between the English-speaking and the French-speaking people. Some people in the province of Quebec want to break away from Canada.

The people of Canada want to solve this problem. They know that to keep Canada united, the French- and English-speaking people need to work together. They need to settle their differences.

Some people in the province of Quebec want to make Quebec a separate country. The poster reads "Yes, it is possible."

When you leave the part of Canada where English is spoken, someone might say "So long" or "Good-bye" to you. But if you leave the part of Canada where French is spoken, the people would say "Au revoir." That is French for "good-bye."

Quick Facts About CANADA

Capital
Ottawa

Borders
Arctic Ocean, Atlantic Ocean, Pacific Ocean, United States

Area
3,851,794 sq. mi
(9,975,376 sq km)

Population
30,675,398

Largest Cities
Toronto (3,863,105 people);
Montreal (3,091,115 people);
Vancouver (1,584,115 people)

Chief crops
wheat, barley, oilseeds, tobacco

Natural resources
nickel, zinc, copper, gold, lead

Longest river
Mackenzie River, at 2,635 miles (4,241 km)

Flag of Canada

▸ **Coastline**
151,492 miles (243,791 km)

Monetary unit
Canadian dollar

Literacy rate
97 percent of Canadians can read and write

Major industries
processed and unprocessed minerals, food products, wood and paper products

Glossary

Calgary Stampede (KAL-guh-ree) A famous rodeo held in the city of Calgary in western Canada

Canadian National (CN) Tower A tall, narrow tower in Toronto that is a popular tourist sight

Château Frontenac (shah-TOW FRON-tih-nak) A very big hotel in Quebec City

federation (fed-uh-RAY-shun) A country that is made up of separate sections

Inuit (IN-yuh-whut) Native people who live in the Arctic area

Jacques Cartier Place (ZHAK kar-TYAY) A popular tourist attraction in the old part of Montreal

Montreal (mon-tree-AWL) A city in eastern Canada that was once the center of the Canadian fur trade

Nôtre-Dame-des-Victoires (NO-truh dam day vik-TWAHR) One of Canada's oldest churches, built in Quebec City in 1688

Nunavut (NOO-nih-vut) Land set aside for Inuits and other Native Americans

Ottawa (AHT-uh-wah) The capital of Canada

parliament Canada's ruling group

parliamentary democracy A government in which the leaders are elected by the people

Place Royale (plahs roy-AHL) The business and shopping section of old Quebec City

prime minister The head of Canada's government

province A section in Canada that is similar to a state in the United States

Quebec City (keh-BEK) The oldest city in Canada

Royal Mounted Police (Mounties) Canada's police force

Toronto (tuh-RONT-oh) The largest Canadian city and the center of English-speaking Canada

Trans-Canada Highway The longest highway in the world, running from east to west across Canada

Vancouver (van-KOO-vur) The largest Canadian city on the Pacific coast

Index

Arctic Ocean 6
Atlantic Ocean 6

Canada Day 24
Canadian National Tower 13
Château Frontenac 10
Christmas 24

Easter 24

France 13

Great Britain 13, 18
Great Lakes 8, 9

Horseshoe Falls 9
Hudson Bay 8

Inuit 14, 20

Jacques Cartier Place 12

Montreal 12

Native Americans 14, 20
Niagara Falls 9
North Pole 6
Nôtre-Dame-des-Victoires 10
Nunavut 14

Ottawa 19

Pacific Ocean 6
parliament 18
Place Royale 10

Quebec City 10

Royal Canadian Mounted Police 18
Russia 6

St. Lawrence River 10

Thanksgiving Day 24
Toronto 13
Trans-Canada Highway 16

United States 6, 8, 16, 24

Vancouver 4, 5